Sept 7, 2001

For Ora —

Damion & Bahlee are happy to have you
as a new friend. They, and I, hope you
enjoy traveling with us in France.

God Bless,

— David J. Schwar

W9-AFU-605

Another Country Calling...

THE ADVENTURES OF SIMON AND BARKLEE™

Simon & Barklee in France

.

David J. Scherer

Illustrations by Kara Richardson

Once, there were two unlikely world travelers. One was Simon T. McTwill, a golden canary with a beautiful voice. The other was Barklee, a frisky terrier with a brave heart. The canary wanted to sing in famous cities around the world, the dog dreamed of adventure. They were the best of friends, and they knew there is no better way to learn about the world and its people than to experience them first hand. So that's what they did . . . they set out to see the world.

E X P L O R E R M E D I A

The Adventure Begins

To begin their journey, Simon and Barklee flew from the United States to England. From there, they took the super-fast Eurostar train that traveled more than 100 miles an hour. Part of the trip was through a tunnel under the waters of the English Channel, which connects the countries of England and France.

As they traveled, Simon and Barklee studied a guidebook to prepare themselves for their introduction to a new country, and to learn a few important words of the beautiful French language.

This is the story of their great adventure in France.

"I had no idea France is so big," said Simon. "Listen to this: It says here that France touches both the Atlantic Ocean and the Mediterranean Sea, and has 59 million people. It has huge mountains—the Pyrenees on the Spanish border, the Alps on the Italian border, and the Jara Mountains that border Switzerland. And it has some of the world's biggest rivers—the Rhine, the Rhone, the Seine and the Loire."

Simon turned the page and named the countries that border France: Germany, Switzerland, Italy, Spain, Belgium and Luxembourg.

"Aren't you forgetting Andorra and Monaco?" said Barklee. "They are tiny countries, but they border France, too."

"You're right. How did you know that?" said Simon.

"I can read, too, y'know." Barklee said, proudly. "I read the guidebook while you were eating a *croissant* in the next car.

As the two talked, their train raced across the countryside. It went so fast that all the fields, farms, villages, cows and cars sped by in a blur.

"What kind of money do they have in France?" Barklee asked.

Simon and Barklee in Paris at the train station.

"They call them *francs*," answered Simon. "And 100 *centimes* equal one franc."

"Does France have a queen, like England?"

"No, France has a president just like we do," replied Simon.

"I've heard that France is a wonderful place. Do you know why?" said Barklee.

"Oh, yes," answered Simon, and he described all the things for which France is famous—art, food, wine, fashions, music, cars, airplanes. Before long, the two of them fell asleep talking as the train brought them closer and closer and closer to France's most famous city: Paris.

"Attention, attention," called the train conductor. "Next stop, Paris."

A few minutes later, a very tired Simon and Barklee arrived at the **Gare du Nord** train station. They gathered up their belongings and stepped into the huge, noisy station. Oh, they were tired. Simon's feathers were drooping and Barklee's tail was dragging.

Simon, I feel like I've been shot out of a circus cannon. Now, with all these people and bags and trains, I'm not sure where to go or what to do next. I can't even hear myself think with all this noise!"

The two weary travelers walked to the middle of the crowded station. An electronic map on the wall displayed the entire Paris subway system, called *Le Metro*. A red arrow on the map showed the visitors where they were, but there was a problem. A big problem.

HOW TO SAY IT, AND WHAT IT MEANS

croissant (kwa-SAHNT)—A flaky French pastry sometimes eaten for breakfast.

francs (frahnks)—French money, both coins and bills.

centimes (sahn-TEEM)—French coins.

Gare du Nord (gar doo nord)—One of several large train stations in Paris.

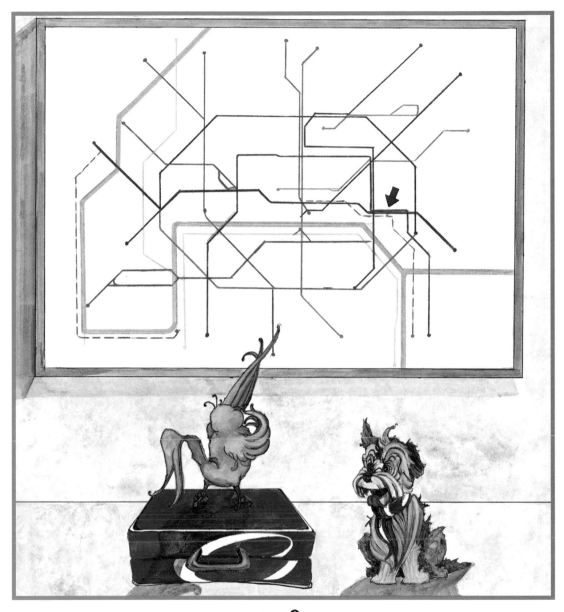

Trying to read the French subway map.

"All the words are in French!" wailed Barklee. "What are we going to do?"

Just then, she felt a gentle tug on her elbow.

"***Excusez-moi***, may I help?" said a small, mouse-like creature with a long tail and funny whiskers. "My name is ***Ratatouille***," he said. "But everybody calls me Ratsy. I am the best tour guide in all of Paris. There are no streets I have not walked. There are no questions that I cannot answer about this beautiful city. There are no . . . "

". . . Do you mind?" Simon said impatiently. "My friend and I are having a private conversation."

"Oh, Simon, keep your feathers on," Barklee said. "Maybe the little guy can help us."

Ratsy smiled, and with a sweep of his paw, removed his **béret** and apologized.

"Forgive me," he said. "I am . . ."

"You're a . . . a . . . you're a rat," said Simon in surprise.

"Yes," he said. "I am a Parisian sewer rat. And we know Paris, the City of Light, better than anyone. I can take you any place you wish to visit. I do not often see my city except at night and under the streets. How I wish to see the beauty of Paris in daylight again!"

The little creature seemed so charming that Simon liked him right away. So, he introduced himself and Barklee and explained that they were visiting France for the first time. Simon said it was his fondest wish to sing at the famous Paris Opera House, which was why Paris was an important stop on their world journey.

"But as you can see," Simon said, "we're lost and we don't speak French. I guess we really could use your help."

"Well, that settles it," Ratsy said, happily. "I will be your tour guide."

And with that, the little rat picked up their bags and led them out of the train station to his car.

"You drive a car?" said Barklee, surprised.

"Yes, of course," said Ratsy. "But it is not as big as the cars in America. The streets here are much narrower, and the cities much older than in your country." He explained that his car was called a **Deux Chevaux**, a small French car whose name means "two horses." Simon and Barklee wondered why a car named for two horses barely had enough room for a canary, a dog and a rat. Ratsy quickly stashed their bag and his small food basket inside. He explained that he frequently got hungry so he always kept his favorite food, **eggplant**, nearby.

"It is delicious," said Ratsy. "Want a bite?"

Barklee didn't like vegetables, let alone purple vegetables. But she was polite.

"Thanks, anyway," she said. "Maybe later."

Ratsy, their french guide, offers them a bite of eggplant.

8

8

HOW TO SAY IT, AND WHAT IT MEANS

excusez-moi (excuse-ay-MWA)—French for
"excuse me."

Ratatouille (rat-at-TOO-ee)—The name of
Simon and Barklee's new friend, and also
the name of a delicious vegetable stew
that includes eggplant.

béret (bur-AY)—A woolen cap with a soft,
flat top.

Deux Chevaux (doo shah-VOH)—A small
French car.

eggplant—A large oval-shaped vegetable that has a purple skin.

In a few moments, Ratsy drove his little car smoothly into traffic, and his new friends were off on a wonderful French adventure.

The Americans were very excited to be in Paris. Simon was so happy, in fact, that while perched on the car's front seat he sang, *"I Love Paris,"* one of his favorite tunes. And Barklee did what dogs always do when they're happy; she stuck her head out the window and barked for joy.

The two visitors waved to everyone.

Like big cities all over the world, the streets of Paris were crowded with cars, buses and motorcycles. Drivers darted this way and that way along the narrow streets, and the sound of horns was everywhere. They were noisier than a gaggle of geese locked in a garage. Simon and Barklee didn't mind, though.

"Now, pay attention, my friends," said Ratsy. "We begin our tour of Paris on the most famous street in the world."

At that moment, he turned his car onto the ***Champs-Elysees***, the longest, widest, most beautiful street Simon and Barklee had ever seen. It was a magnificent ***boulevard*** that stretched for more than a mile. On both sides were tall, splendid trees, fancy shops and outdoor restaurants with bright canvas

Simon giving Barklee a bird's-eye view of the Champs-Elysees.

awnings hanging over the sidewalk. So many, many people everywhere. Thousands of people were enjoying the warm, sunny afternoon, walking, talking, eating, jogging, sitting, taking pictures, pushing baby carriages, buying souvenirs and looking in shop windows.

Simon and Barklee had never seen such a beautiful sight. Simon got so excited he suddenly swooped Barklee high into the air over the fabulous street for a bird's eye view.

"Wow," said Simon.

"Cool," said Barklee.

HOW TO SAY IT, AND WHAT IT MEANS

Champs-Elysees (shomps ay-lay-ZAY)—
The widest boulevard in Paris, and one
of the most famous streets in the world.

boulevard—A broad street lined with trees.

Did I not I tell you?" said Ratsy. "Is this not the most beautiful boulevard you have ever seen? And did you know, the words boulevard and restaurant are French words?"

"Oh, really?" said Barklee, winking at Simon, "I thought they were American words."

Ratsy looked a little insulted for a moment, and then he laughed at Barklee's kidding.

As they drove up the boulevard, Simon and Barklee suddenly saw a large, stone archway in the distance. It was huge, and grew bigger the closer they got.

When they stopped in front of it, they couldn't believe their eyes.

It was a monument larger and taller than any building nearby, and it stood over the Champs-Elysees like a two-legged giant.

"Oh, my," said Barklee, her mouth hanging open as she looked up.

"My friends," said Ratsy, "welcome to the *Arc de Triomphe*. It is one of

The Arc de Triomphe has some of the worst traffic in Paris.

France's greatest monuments. It is made of stone and is dedicated to the brave soldiers of France and the many battles they fought. It is almost 46 meters high and 41 meters wide." Simon and Barklee looked at each other in confusion. Ratsy quickly explained. "We measure things differently here. We use the metric system. In your way of measuring, it is 150 feet high and 135 feet wide. At night, with thousands of lights shining on it, it looks as if it were made of gold."

Ratsy said the Arc de Triomphe is one of the most beautiful sights in Paris, but it also has the worst traffic.

He pointed to the river of cars, trucks, buses and motorcycles winding around the monument from 12 different streets. It would be Simon and Barklee's next big adventure.

"Here we go," shouted Ratsy. He suddenly steered his little car into the flow and rode around the monument three times. It was a wild ride. Simon felt like a cork on a giant wave. Ratsy was a good driver, but he was so busy being a tour guide he almost hit a bus.

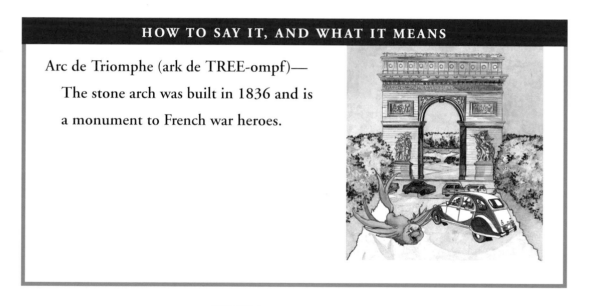

HOW TO SAY IT, AND WHAT IT MEANS

Arc de Triomphe (ark de TREE-ompf)—
**The stone arch was built in 1836 and is
a monument to French war heroes.**

Where shall we go now?" he said.

"The opera house," said Simon. "Yes," said Barklee, "take us to the Paris Opera House so we can hear Simon sing."

So, off they went.

The city of Paris has two opera houses. One is new, the other is old. But Simon and Barklee wanted adventure, so Ratsy chose the old opera house for one very good reason: "They say it is haunted!" he said, "haunted by a man no one has ever seen . . . the **Phantom** of the Opera."

The old Paris Opera House might possibly be haunted.

Simon felt the feathers rise on the back of his neck. A ghost? A phantom? Here? In Paris? Simon and Barklee looked at each other in silent wonder.

When they arrived, the front door was locked. So, Ratsy started back to the car. "Let's see if we can find another way in," said Simon. "I didn't come all this way to be stopped now. I want everybody at home to know I sang at the Paris Opera House."

So, the three of them walked warily down a dark, creepy alley. They found a side door. It was slightly open, almost as though they were expected. They pushed hard on the door, and it opened with a weird creaking sound.

"C'mon, guys," whispered Simon, "what are you afraid of? Let's go in."

With Simon in the lead, they all tiptoed inside. The old opera house was as dark and quiet as a graveyard, which made them even more scared. A thousand empty seats hid in the shadows. It was spooky. Very spooky. Barklee was on the alert. She had a dog's sharp senses and felt something strange was lurking nearby.

Ratsy, too, felt danger. He looked up at the high ceiling. Did he imagine it, or were there eyes peering down at them?

Only Simon was able to put aside his fears.

He had come all the way from America to sing. So, unafraid, he stood on the opera house stage and began. Simon's first notes were a little off-key because his tongue was a bit dry. He began again. As he warmed up, though, he did not see the two wicked yellow eyes fixed on him from the darkness.

The eyes belonged to a creature hunched for an attack.

"Simon!" Barklee yelled suddenly. "Let's get out of here. Now! I have a bad feeling about this place. C'mon, we're leaving."

Back outside, the three laughed nervously at how spooky it was inside the opera house.

"I'm hungry," said Barklee, "let's get something to eat."

"Yes," Ratsy said, "I know a nice little outdoor café."

"No, not yet," said Simon, "I'm going back. I want to do what I came to do. Sing!"

And before Barklee and Ratsy could stop him, Simon flew back down the alley and through the door from which they had just escaped.

Once again, he stood on the opera house stage preparing to sing.

Just then, something moved in the darkness.

"Is that you, Barklee? Ratsy?" Simon called out. No answer. "Hey, guys, have a seat." Still no answer. He began to tremble from his tail feathers to his beak.

*S*uddenly, an enormous cat with a zigzag scar between his angry yellow eyes leaped from the shadows, trapping the canary between its claws. Simon was dreadfully sorry that he had left the safety of his

Simon is stalked by the cat.

friends. But just as he was about to become lunch, the cat cried out. Out of nowhere, a tall man in a mask and black cape had grabbed the cat by its neck as it squirmed and hissed and fought to break free. The man flung the animal into the shadows and it scurried off with a scream and a clatter.

Simon lay dazed and breathless on the stage floor. His mind was reeling in terror.

"You were lucky, young fellow" said the mysterious figure. "Another moment and I would have been too late." He picked Simon up and perched him gently on his hand.

"Who . . . who are you?" Simon said in a *quavering* voice.

I think you know who I am."

"You're the . . . the Phantom of . . ."

Just then, they heard Barklee and Ratsy running in from the alley.

"Wait, sir, don't leave," Simon said.

He quickly flew to greet them and began telling about being rescued from the evil cat. But when they returned, the stage was empty.

"He's gone," said Simon, looking all around, "and I didn't even get to thank him."

"Who?" said Ratsy.

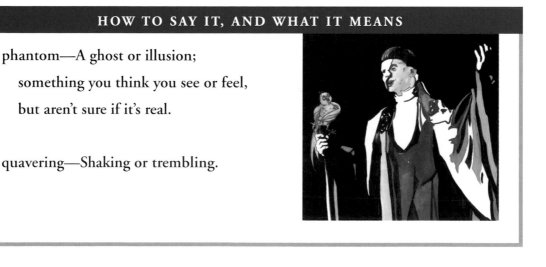

HOW TO SAY IT, AND WHAT IT MEANS

phantom—A ghost or illusion;
    something you think you see or feel,
    but aren't sure if it's real.

quavering—Shaking or trembling.

Simon is saved by the Phantom of the Opera.

"The Phantom of the Opera," said Simon.

"Oh, sure," said Barklee, "that's just a ghost story they tell to kids. There's no such thing as a phantom of the opera. C'mon, let's get some lunch. I'm hungry."

Simon looked back again at the empty stage, then followed his friends.

Ratsy drove them to the *Oo-La-La Café*, a typical outdoor French restaurant. Since Simon and Barklee couldn't read French, they decided to choose what sounded good. It seemed like another adventure. So, Simon ordered **crêpes**, and Barklee chose something called **escargots**.

Barklee eating escargots at the Oo-la-la Café.

"I'll have escargots," Barklee told the waiter, practicing her French.

It was delicious. She cleaned her plate and might have asked for seconds. That is, until Ratsy explained that escargots are snails cooked in garlic butter.

"Snails?" she said, looking a little pale. "Crawly snails? Oh yuk! Next time, Ratsy, you order for all of us. Just remember, no eggplant."

After lunch, Simon hopped up on the café table and burst into a song. He sang "**Frère Jacques**," a favorite song of French children. It means "Brother John."

"**Merci beaucoup**," Ratsy cried, clapping happily. "Oh, **Monsieur** Simon, you sing the most delightful songs."

Ratsy couldn't remember when he had such a good time. He had been with the two Americans only a few hours and he felt like they were old friends already. He offered to be their tour guide wherever they traveled in France.

"It's a deal," said Simon, shaking Ratsy's paw. "But first we want to see more of Paris."

After all the excitement of the morning, they agreed to have a quiet afternoon. So, the three boarded a tour boat to float down the Seine River.

HOW TO SAY IT, AND WHAT IT MEANS

crêpes (kreps)—A French pastry; a thin pancake rolled and filled with jam or cheese.

escargots (ess-cahr-GO)—A French delicacy; edible snails cooked in garlic butter.

Frère Jacques (FRER-ah ZHAHK-ah)— A favorite song of French children.

Merci beaucoup (mare-SEE boh-KOO)— French for "thank you very much."

Monsieur (meh-SYUR)—French for "mister."

Ratsy, Simon and Barklee cruising down the Seine.

The Seine is very wide and winds through Paris like a giant ribbon. Almost everything that makes Paris beautiful and popular can be seen while drifting along the banks of the river.

Notre Dame with its flying buttresses.

At one point, Ratsy pointed out the **Louvre**, one of the world's oldest, biggest and greatest art museums. It contains so many important paintings and sculpture, he said, that it would take someone days to see everything.

Farther down the river, Simon and Barklee saw the **Notre Dame** Cathedral,

Gazing at the tall Eiffel Tower from their tour boat.

one of the largest, most beautiful churches in Europe, standing on a small island in the middle of the Seine.

"There's something strange about the cathedral," Barklee said.

"You're right, Barklee," said the tour boat captain. "You see those wing-like pillars on the side of the cathedral? Those pillars are called 'flying buttresses,' and they are designed to strengthen the heavy stone walls." The captain said the pillars seem to be working because Notre Dame is still standing after more than 700 years!

Farther on, they spotted the famous ***Tour Eiffel***. It is 275 meters, or 900 feet tall. It is so tall that Simon and Barklee nearly fell backwards trying to see the top. Ratsy said the tower was built more than 100 years ago by a French engineer named Gustave Eiffel, and even has elevators that go all the way to the top.

HOW TO SAY IT, AND WHAT IT MEANS

Louvre (loovr)—The museum, one of the most famous in the world, is a former French palace that was built on the banks of the Seine.

Notre Dame (NO-trah dahm)—The old cathedral is open to visitors seven days a week and has organ recitals in the evening.

Tour Eiffel (Toor ee-FELL)—In English it is called the Eiffel Tower.

As the three left the tour boat, Ratsy spoke up.

"Well, where shall we go now?"

"I'm hungry again," said Barklee.

"You're always hungry," Simon said, laughing.

"I have a good idea," said Ratsy. "Let us have a picnic. France is famous for its picnics."

So, they went to a neighborhood market, picked up some snacks, and drove to the **Bois du Boulogne**, the biggest and most beautiful park in Paris. Ratsy pointed to a grassy area underneath a big, shady

Sharing a baguette at the Bois du Boulogne.

tree, and spread a blanket. "This is my favorite spot to loaf with some bread," he said with a little chuckle. He had brought a long, skinny loaf of bread called a **baguette**, some fruit, fresh cheese and a jug of apple cider. And, of course, Ratsy brought out some eggplant to nibble on.

"Want to try some of my eggplant now, Barklee?" Ratsy asked.

"Oh, maybe later, Ratsy."

Soon, they were all busy eating and drinking. After all, being a tourist is hungry work. Then, they fell asleep for a nap.

HOW TO SAY IT, AND WHAT IT MEANS

Bois du Boulogne (bwa doo-ball-OWN)—
The largest, most beautiful park in Paris.

baguette (bag-ET)—A long, skinny loaf
of French bread.

When they woke, Ratsy told Simon and Barklee that if they really wanted a good view of Paris they should climb the steep path to the top of the hill of **Montmartre**.

"Simon," said Barklee, "hop onto my shoulder and we'll race Ratsy up the hill!"

"Ah, but there is nothing so fast as a French sewer rat," Ratsy said, accepting the challenge. "But, if you insist. . . . "

With that, the trio scampered to the top of the hill. From there they could see many old narrow streets and squares, quite unlike the ones at home. Tourists

Viewing the french countryside of Normandy.

were watching sidewalk artists paint pictures of little scenes of Paris. France is a wonderful place for artists. Its natural beauty has attracted them for longer than anyone can remember. Some of the artists were even painting pictures of the people who were watching them paint.

After some more exploring, Simon and Barklee went with Ratsy to a small hotel to settle for the night. They would need a good sleep after such a busy day.

Next morning, the three set off on a journey west to the Normandy coast. It is a well-known farm region along the edge of the English Channel and famous throughout France for its dairy products and apples. Armies from many different countries invaded Normandy for hundreds of years. During the middle of the 20th Century, the American military forces came to Normandy to help free France from German invaders in World War II.

The destruction of war has been removed. However, a very beautiful but *somber* American cemetery is there to remind visitors of the cost of war. Fortunately, Normandy is once again a very charming part of France.

As Ratsy's little car puttered along the narrow roads, they passed dairy cows, herds of goats, and saw farmers in black wool berets and denim overalls planting their crops by hand. French landowners have plowed the same way for centuries to produce delicious garden-fresh food.

As the adventurers put together another picnic lunch, they learned something about the languages of Europe. The French like to use long words while Americans prefer shorter ones. The travelers bought freshly baked bread from a village ***boulangerie***, which means bakery. Then they stuffed two sausages into their sack at the butcher shop, which is called a ***charcutèrie***.

"It's fun to learn new words," said Barklee, "but new foods are something else. From now on, I'm not eating anything slimy or that crawls on the ground."

Simon laughed uproariously. "Didn't you like your escargots?"

For their meal, the trio wandered around the outdoor market, selecting bread, fruit, fresh cheese and freshly squeezed grape juice. They paid for their groceries with francs, and were given centimes in change. It was a good way for the visitors to learn more about French money.

After picking up their picnic goodies, they spread their blanket beside a small river to eat. Once rested, they were ready to see more of the beautiful countryside.

"Have you noticed," said Ratsy, "that most French villages have churches in the center of town? It is because the market square in front of the church is where the local people like to meet their friends and tell stories." He said it is here that the older men play an outdoor game that is like our bowling. They call it **boules**.

HOW TO SAY IT, AND WHAT IT MEANS

Montmartre (mohnt MAR-trah)—A
    section of Paris popular with tourists,
    and the only hill in the city.

somber—sad.

boulangerie (bo-LONJ-eerie)—French
    for bakery.

charcutèrie (char-COOT-eerie)—French
    for butcher shop.

boules (bool)—An outdoor game like
    bowling, popular in France.

Back on the road again, the trio arrived at the site of an ancient church, or abbey, called Mont-Saint Michel. It is 800 years old and sits like a fortress atop a hill just off the coast. The abbey is connected to the mainland by a two-lane road, and when the tide is out, it is easy to drive to it. But when the tide comes in, the road is covered by the sea.

On the day the three travelers arrived, Ratsy parked his car in the abbey

Driving to Mont-Saint Michel when the tide is out.

parking lot. Unfortunately, no one read the warning sign. Otherwise, they would have known that the tide would soon put the parking lot under water.

That afternoon, Simon and Barklee spent the day exploring old buildings and souvenir shops below the abbey. They stopped for tea and pastries and wrote postcards to their friends in America.

When they returned to the abbey, Barklee looked out to the sea.

Ratsy's little car floating out to sea.

"Uh oh," she said, with a worried voice.

"What is it?" said Ratsy.

"Look out there," she said, pointing. "Isn't that your car out there in the ocean?"

"Eeek!" shrieked Ratsy, running frantically out of the abbey and racing down the long hill crying, "My car! My little car! It is sailing to England!"

Just then, a monk from the abbey, dressed in a brown robe and sandals, came outside to see what all the noise was about. He looked out to sea and smiled.

"Oh, do not worry, **mon ami**," he said. "Your car will return with the tide. What goes out always comes in. Come, bring your friends and stay the night with us. Your car will surely be here when you get up tomorrow morning."

"Are you sure, Monsieur Monk?" Ratsy asked, gasping for breath.

"Yes," the monk answered calmly. "We know these things."

Sure enough, the morning tide returned the floating car back to the parking lot. It was wet, and bits of seaweed draped around the bumpers. But otherwise the little Deux Chevaux was in good shape. Ratsy was one happy rat. Soon after, the three travelers packed up their car and were back on the road.

My idea of floating," Ratsy said, "is a hot-air balloon ride across the Loire Valley. That is where the best ballooning is in France."

At this suggestion, Simon's eyes opened with excitement. Barklee let out an excited yelp. "A real balloon adventure?" she asked. "Awesome! Let's go!"

On the way, Ratsy explained that the Loire Valley is one of the most beautiful regions in France. It has many small rivers, streams and canals that run together to become the Loire River, and along the river are elegant castles called **châteaux**. Ratsy said the chateaux were built hundreds of years ago by French kings and other members of the French nobility. When the three arrived at the Loire Valley, Ratsy found just what he was looking for.

On the outskirts of the little town of St. Aignan, on the Cher River, Ratsy spotted a huge bright red, yellow, and blue balloon. They arrived just in time because the pilot, Pierre Propane, was making preparations to take off. He invited them aboard, and, moments later, the balloon was filled with heated air and rose as gently as a leaf on the wind.

Ratsy guides his friends in a balloon.

Their balloon sailed higher and higher and higher, and soon they were hundreds of feet over the tallest rooftop. It turned out that Ratsy was as good a guide in the air as he was on the ground.

"Look down there," he said. "That is the city of Tours."

Just then, the air around them was filled with a sweet, wonderful perfume.

"What's that heavenly smell?" asked Barklee, taking a big sniff of air.

"That is the scent of vineyards," said Ratsy. He explained that the vineyards grow grapes from which France produces some of the most famous wines in the world. He told them that the vines were brought to France by the Romans more than 2,000 years ago, at a time when France was known as Gaul.

As the balloon drifted, the three passengers enjoyed their own silent thoughts. Barklee dreamed of running through the forest below, chasing squirrels, looking for bones, and doing whatever else dogs do on a sunny day. Simon imagined himself as the famous **Marquis de Musique**, living in one of the magnificent chateaux and singing for the royalty of Europe. Ratsy just enjoyed the view and the company of his friends. He tried to memorize everything he saw because he knew it would not be long before he would be back under the streets of Paris.

As they sailed above the Loire Valley, they saw a large canal **barge** floating slowly toward the biggest and finest chateau they had seen. Pierre told them it was called the **Château de Chenonceaux**. It seemed to lean right over the river and looked like a floating castle.

Barklee was watching the barge float closer and closer to the beautiful building. Suddenly, she yelped, "Oh, no! The barge is going to run right into the château!"

But as the balloon drew nearer, the passengers could see the château was built right across the river. Instead of hitting the château, the barge floated beneath it.

"Boy, that scared me for a minute," said Barklee. "I was sure there was going to be an accident."

In time, the thrill of ballooning was replaced with another feeling: hunger. So, after landing back on the ground, the trio bid Pierre **adieu** and headed for the city of Tours for lunch.

HOW TO SAY IT, AND WHAT IT MEANS

mon ami (mohn a-MEE)—French for
"my friend."

château and châteaux (shat-TOE)—A
beautiful big house that looks like a
castle. When the word ends in 'x', it
means more than one house.

Marquis (mar-KEE)—A French nobleman.

Château de Chenonceaux (chen-an-SO)—
One of the many fine, old chateaux in the Loire region.

barge (barj)—A flat-bottomed boat used to carry heavy freight up and down
the river.

adieu (ah-DYOU)—French for "goodbye."

While they were eating, Simon happened to overhear two villagers talking about something called *truffles*, and how hard it is to find them in the Perigord Forest.

"If we could get some," whispered one of the villagers, "we could be rich."

Simon suddenly got a terrific idea: If he and his friends found some of these truffles on their own, they could make lots of money. He told the others, and they all thought it was a wonderful plan.

"But how do you catch a truffle?" asked Barklee.

"Yes," said Ratsy. "Do they run very fast?"

"Don't you guys know anything?" said Simon, shaking his head. "If you're going to catch truffles, you need some rope and a butterfly net." So, they bought their supplies and drove south to the Perigord Forest.

The next day, the three arrived in the forest. Simon went looking for a place to set up camp while the other two unloaded the car.

The trio set out with rope and a butterfly net to catch truffles.

Suddenly, Simon heard the strangest sound he ever heard—a low, growling, grunting sound. *A wild truffle*, he wondered? He searched high and low, left and right, but didn't see anything.

Then, just when he thought he imagined the noise, Simon heard it again. This time it was so close that he shook with fear. He flew back to the car as fast as he could and told the others. Simon looked like he was going to faint, and Ratsy looked around for a hiding place.

"I'm not afraid of a truffle," said Barklee, with a firm voice. "I don't care how big it is or how fast it runs."

"What shall we do?" said Ratsy, who was ready to drive back to Paris immediately.

"Relax, everybody. I have a plan," said Barklee. "The truffle doesn't know we're here, so we'll catch it by surprise."

She persuaded Simon to take her and Ratsy back to the spot where he heard the truffle. From there, the three daring hunters crept through the forest, careful not to talk. No one made a peep until Barklee accidentally stepped on Ratsy's tail.

"Ahhgh!" Ratsy yipped.

"Oops, sorry," she said.

"Shush!" Simon hissed.

As they crept forward, they all suddenly heard the loud groaning, grunting sound. The truffle! It was hiding in a bush less than 10 feet away! Simon grabbed Barklee and tried to pull her away. Ratsy grabbed the butterfly net and ran in circles. Only Barklee stood her ground, sniffing and pawing at the ground in front of the bushes.

HOW TO SAY IT, AND WHAT IT MEANS

truffle—A small mushroom-like food that grows underground and looks like a walnut.

Jules LePorc looking for truffles.

C-c-come out w-where I can s-s-see you," she stammered, a little afraid. "I know y-you are in there so c-come out!"

Suddenly, out of the bushes came a plump, smiling, four-legged creature with pointed ears, a long snout, and a round, pink body.

"***Bonjour, mon amis!***" said the creature with a friendly grunt. "Are you lost? Do you need help finding your way out of the forest?"

Barklee was stunned. She stood staring at something that looked very familiar. Confused, she blurted, "You're not a truffle!"

"Snorffle, snorffle, grunt, grunt," the bulky animal chuckled. "Of course not. I am ***Jules LePorc***, a . . . how do you Americans say? . . . a pig."

Ratsy and Simon stared in astonishment. A pig!

HOW TO SAY IT, AND WHAT IT MEANS

Bonjour, mon amis (bone-ZHUR, mohn a-MEEZ)—French for, "Good day, my friends."

Jules LePorc (zhule lay-PORK)—The name of a truffle-hunting pig.

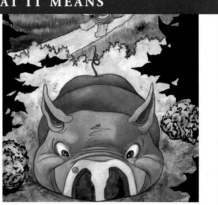

J ules looked at the net Ratsy was holding.

"Are you searching for butterflies, mon amis?" he asked.

"No," said Simon, "we want to catch truffles so we can make lots of money."

"What a wonderful bit of luck!" said Jules. "I, too, am looking for truffles. But you will not need a butterfly net."

"Have you ever seen a truffle?" said Barklee.

"But of course," said Jules, who explained that a truffle is not a beast to be hunted. A truffle is a small, lumpy food about the size of a walnut that grows in the ground near oak trees.

"They look something like mushrooms," Jules said. "and they are very, very expensive. Only the finest chefs use them to flavor their favorite dishes. It is a ***gastronomical*** treasure that one would enjoy in a very special dinner."

Jules said he had a "nose" for truffle hunting, and demonstrated how he used his snout to smell truffles underground, and then to dig them out. It took almost three hours to find just two of them, and he dropped them into Simon's basket.

"I wonder," he said, "if I might join you for a picnic. I am very hungry now. But then a pig is always hungry."

Jules joins Ratsy, Simon and Barklee for a gastronomical picnic.

"Well, please join us," said Simon. "We have a baguette, some cider, some *camembert* cheese from Normandy, some apples from the Loire, and . . . "

"*Bon, bon*," Jules said happily.

" . . . And eggplant, too," Ratsy quickly added.

"Humph," said Jules. "I do not think so, Monsieur Ratsy. I do not eat purple food!"

After a tasty picnic, the group rested. All that remained were the two large, black, raw truffles. Jules offered one of them to Barklee. Of course, after her experience with escargots, she was not about to put one of those lumpy, muddy things in her mouth.

"But you must understand, Mademoiselle Barklee," Jules said. "This truffle, with all its little bumps, is a thing of great taste. In France, we call it the 'black diamond' of cooking."

Jules walked them back to their car.

"So now, my friends, if you want a real eating adventure, you must go south to Avignon in Provence," he said. "There you will find the restaurant *Boeuf et*

HOW TO SAY IT, AND WHAT IT MEANS

gastronomical—The custom and style of good eating.

camembert (cam-em-BEHR)—One of many fine French cheeses.

bon (bohn)—French for "good."

Boeuf et Oeuf (bouf et oof)—French for "beef and egg," and is also the name of the restaurant that Simon and Barklee visited.

Ducs DuBois (dooks du BWA)—The name of the chef recommended by Jules LePorc.

Au revoir (oh re-VWA)—French for "goodbye."

Oeuf and my friend, the chef, **Ducs DuBois**. He will prepare for you the finest dish you have ever eaten."

"That sounds good to me," said Barklee, wagging her tail. "I'm ready for an eating adventure."

"Oh, Barklee," laughed Simon. "You never get enough to eat."

With that, Jules called *"Au revoir!"* and lumbered back into the bushes.

For the next few hours, Ratsy drove Simon and Barklee through green hills and valleys, across rivers and streams, past farms, fields, and ancient villages. They all agreed the trip to Avignon took them through some of the prettiest countryside they had ever seen.

Simon takes his friends for a quick flight to see Avignon.

From time to time on the drive, Simon studied the guidebook while Barklee kept her head out the window, enjoying the breeze on her fur.

"Are we there yet?" she said happily.

"Almost," said Simon.

Simon loved reading about new places. From reading the guidebook, he learned that Avignon is a historic city. It was built two thousand years ago on the banks of the Rhone River near the Mediterranean Sea. Once it was a center of Roman culture. Today its warm summers and mild winters make it popular with tourists and artists. Simon also learned that Avignon, like many Roman cities, was built behind high walls and guard towers to defend against invaders. Avignon boasts 39 towers which are connected by stone walls around the old city. It even has a hilltop palace—the ***Palais des Papes***—that was the Pope's summer home hundreds of years ago.

Just then, Ratsy's little car rounded a curve in the road.

"There it is!" shouted Barklee. "There's Avignon."

Simon laughed.

"Barklee," he said, "I never met anyone who loved adventure more than you." With that, he took Barklee and Ratsy for a quick flight to see the ancient city and ruins from the air.

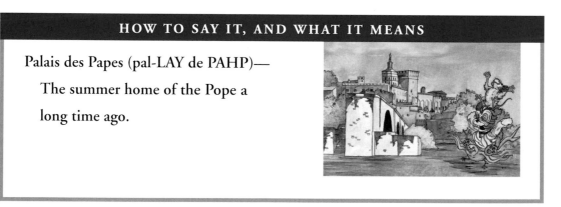

HOW TO SAY IT, AND WHAT IT MEANS

Palais des Papes (pal-LAY de PAHP)—
The summer home of the Pope a
long time ago.

Ratsy parked his little Deux Chevaux outside one of the city's ancient gates, and they went in search of the restaurant that Jules

Chef Ducs preparing a galantine with truffles.

had recommended. They found it near Avignon's busy town square and a crowded open-air market.

Ratsy said French chefs take their cooking very seriously. He said the French do not care what the food is, or what it looks like before it is cooked. But it must thrill the taste buds when it is eaten. They use only the best and freshest ingredients found in the local markets.

Like many of the best French restaurants, the Boeuf et Oeuf was small and elegant. Barklee looked at the crisp white linen napkins on the table with the beautiful plates and fancy silverware. Then she whispered to Simon, "I can't eat in a fancy restaurant. I'm not dressed for it. Besides, the day is too beautiful for us to be inside."

Simon agreed, and, in his most polite manner, asked Chef Ducs if he could prepare something with the truffles for a picnic lunch instead. The chef quickly agreed. *"Oui, oui,"* he said. "I will prepare for you my special *galantine* of mallard, flecked with your truffles, fresh pork fat, *pistachio nuts*, and ham. While it is cooking, you shop in our lively market for the rest of your picnic. Come back in one hour."

HOW TO SAY IT, AND WHAT IT MEANS

oui (we)—French for "yes."

galantine—A delicious meal of boned meat with a variety of spices and other ingredients.

pistachio nuts—A small, tasty nut that comes from a pistachio tree.

For the next hour, Simon, Barklee and Ratsy went shopping in the open-air market. The wooden stalls burst with fresh fruits, vegetables, cheeses, breads, and all kinds of meat and fish. They even saw fresh octopus that had been taken from the depths of the Mediterranean Sea—but they did not buy any.

Ratsy squeezing fruits and vegetables in the open-air market.

Meanwhile, Ratsy was squeezing and poking fruits and vegetables he wanted in their basket. Suddenly, one vendor shouted: "You! Monsieur Whiskers! No more squeezing my fruit! You make everything flat! Buy first, then squeeze!" Barklee and Ratsy skipped away, giggling. Simon was terribly embarrassed.

The trio skipped back to the Boeuf et Oeuf and collected the galantine. Oh, how good it smelled! "***Bon appétit!***" called Chef DuBois as they hurried out the door.

"***Merci***," the three called back in return and walked back to their car, carrying their baskets. One by one, they piled all the food into Ratsy's car and headed into the flower-drenched hills above Avignon.

HOW TO SAY IT, AND WHAT IT MEANS

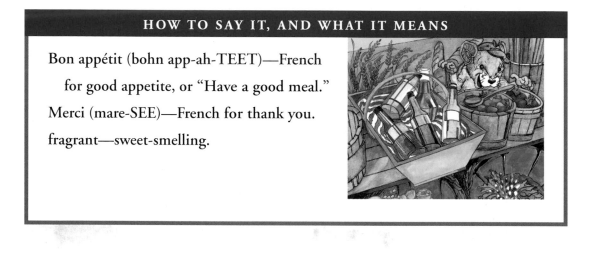

Bon appétit (bohn app-ah-TEET)—French
    for good appetite, or "Have a good meal."
Merci (mare-SEE)—French for thank you.
fragrant—sweet-smelling.

Thee they wandered among the sun-covered fields until they found the perfect spot for lunch. It had to be perfect because Simon and Barklee knew this would be their last day in France and their last French picnic for a while.

After a lazy lunch, the three friends sat quietly in the ***fragrant*** meadow.

Simon, Barklee and Ratsy had been through so much together in such a short time—their driving adventure at the Arc de Triomphe, the danger at the Paris Opera House, the pleasure of floating down the Seine River, the excitement at Mont-St. Michel, and the fun of hunting truffles and ballooning over the Loire Valley.

"You must come back," Ratsy said, already missing his new friends. "There is so much of France I want to show you. I want to take you to the cliffs of Dieppe, the beaches of Bretagne, the ancient city of Strasbourg, and then we can all go skiing at Mont Blanc in the French Alps."

We will return to your beautiful country.

R atsy," asked Simon, "what will you do when we leave? Stay in Paris?"

"Oh, maybe for a little while," said Ratsy. "I think maybe I will come back to Avignon. It is very pretty here, and Chef DuBois says I can work at his restaurant." Ratsy said he has many eggplant recipes that he knows everyone will love to eat.

HOW TO SAY IT, AND WHAT IT MEANS

magnifique (man-ye-FEEK)—French for "magnificent" or "wonderful."

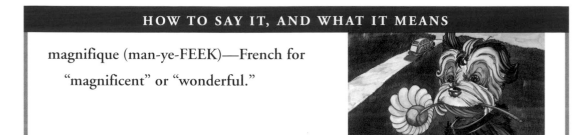

Before the last rays of the sun disappeared, Simon sang a sweet song of farewell. He and Barklee were grateful for their friendship with Ratatouille, the little French sewer rat.

"Oh, what a beautiful country," sighed Barklee.

"Oh, oui," agreed Simon. "We will return. There is so much to see and taste and learn here—and everywhere. Travel and learning about our world and meeting fascinating people are, well, *magnifique!*"

■ ■ ■

MORE EASY FRENCH WORDS

bonsoir (bon-SWAH)—good evening

bibliotèque (beeb-lee-oh-TEK)— library

école (e-COAL)—school

frère (frayre)—brother

la femme (la fem)—girl

le garçon (leu gar-SOHN)—boy

Madam (ma-DAM)—Mrs.

maison (may-SOHN)—house

maitre (MAY-trah)—teacher

mere (mare)—mother

non (noh)—no

père (pear)—father

soeur (sir)—sister

COUNTING IN FRENCH

Un (uhn)—one

Deux (doo)—two

Trois (twah)—three

Quartre (QWA-trah)—four

Cinq (sank)—five

Six (sees)—six

Sept (set)—seven

Huit (wheat)—eight

Neuf (newf)—nine

Dix (dees)—ten

For my grandchildren
Casey, Kyle, and Nicole

■

Text and illustrations Copyright © 2001 David J. Scherer
All rights reserved

An ExplorerMedia book 2001 by David J. Scherer
Produced in association with Niche Press/Seattle

Rights: All rights reserved. No part of this book may be reproduced or utilized in any
form or by any means, electronic or mechanical, including photocopying, recording,
electronic transfer, or by information storage and retrieval systems, without permission in
writing from the publisher, except by a book reviewer who may quote brief passages in a
review. Inquiries or communications to the author should be directed to: ExplorerMedia,
a division of Simon and Barklee, Inc., 2280 E. Whidbey Shores Rd., Langley WA (USA)
98260; (360) 730-2360.

To order additional copies and accompanying educational materials, call or visit our web
site: www.SimonandBarklee.com

Cataloging-in-Publication Data:

Scherer, David J.
        Simon and Barklee in France / author, David J. Scherer ; illus by Kara
Richardson. — 1st ed.
        p.   cm. — (another country calling, the adventures of Simon and Barklee.)
        American travelers Simon and Barklee visit France, where their fun-filled
adventures introduce them to the geography, history, and culture of a beautiful country.
        ISBN: 0-9704-661-0-2
        1. France—Juvenile literature.   2. France—History—Juvenile literature
    3. France—social life and customs—Juvenile literature.   I. Title.

DC17.S34 2001   944
                                                                                    QB100-794

Illustrations by Kara Richardson
Designed and typeset by Elizabeth Watson

Printed in Singapore by Star Standard Industries (S) Pte Ltd